AQUARIUS

AQUARIUS

AQUARIUS

AQUARIUS

每個人心中都有一座島嶼,

藉文字呼息而靜謐,

Island,我們心靈的岸。

無名人
Nobody

愛莉絲・歐思華 Alice Oswald 著
陳育虹 譯

國際好評

這是一首海的無名抒情詩。它帶著《俄瑞斯忒亞》與《斐洛克特底》兩部古希臘劇的暗流，徹底重新解讀、敘述了《奧德賽》……《無名人》對「甚麼是凡夫」有所省思；它打破了時空，感傷、聳人且氣勢磅礴。

——羅珊娜・華倫，詩人

悸動人心……《無名人》如神話而寫實，既古典又現代……歐思華正處於她創作的高峰。

——《觀察報》凱特・柯樂薇

這是一篇為水而寫，為語文的流動，也為人與故事的間隙而寫的詩……讀《無名人》的感受在事後仍縈繞心中。

——《財經時報》瑪麗亞・柯若芙

出人意表的文字如湧，讓人驚異……這是音節與意象的快旋舞，技巧完美無缺。《無名人》是歐思華在形式上最自由的作品，一些零星低語集聚，是為尋覓一新耳目的創意。

——《週日時報》傑瑞米・諾爾・陶德

一個革新者，生態詩人，她的構思活潑，帶著感官經驗。這些似乎矛盾的內容，創造出獨特的迴響與迫切感，昇華了詩本身……《無名人》是某種小說詩，它甚且抗拒以傳統方式說故事。

——《衛報》費歐娜・桑普生

【譯序】
詩的深海

●

詩,該往哪個方向發展?詩人能如何自我突破?

從一開始,拓造新局似乎就是歐思華為自己設定的創作目標。

愛莉絲・歐思華(Alice Oswald, 1966-)生於英國柏克郡。在牛津大學主修英國文學並拿到博士學位後,她未走學術路線而選擇創作。由於從小跟隨任職「皇室庭園設計師」的母親身邊,耳濡目染下也嫻熟花草,她決定去「皇家園藝學會」上課,取得證照,成為專業園藝師。蒔花弄草能讓腦子空出來,是詩人的理想工作,她說;而這園藝專長在日後也確實支撐了她的創作夢。但雖是園藝家,她自家院子卻雜草叢生蟲屍處處,蘋果樹下的爛蘋果和破羽球網糾結一團,因為她寧可保持生態不受干擾。她的書房掛著水獺皮,是前輩詩人泰德・休斯的遺物。

在書房,除了不時翻閱厚達兩千多頁的山繆・詹森《牛津國家人物傳記大辭典》,歐思華對密爾頓情有獨鍾,曾帶領社區社團演出《失樂園》。她也十分喜愛貝克特,說他是「躲在針孔後的劇作家」,創造出一間語言的暗室,讓光從暗室穿透。——她偏愛戲劇也有淵源:在大學社團演出莎劇時,她與先生歐彼德(Peter Oswald)相識,歐彼德後來成了知名劇作家,曾任莎士比亞劇院駐院劇作家多年。

出版了八本詩集,帶大三個孩子之後,2019 年她終於重回母校,擔任第四十六任「牛津詩歌教授」。這榮譽職位設於 1708 年,人選由牛津校友投票決定,之前受聘的有奧登、希尼等前輩;歐

思華是三百年來獲選的第一位女性。「詩歌教授」任期四年，職責是每學期做一場演講。她的講題包括〈剝蝕的藝術〉、〈訪談水〉、〈國王在夢中〉、〈哀悼地球〉、〈詩的生與死〉等。

　　從這些講題，從歐思華人生不同階段的抉擇，我們多少可看出她的生命關注和傾向：大自然，文學，生死冥想。

●

　　歐思華1996年出版的第一本詩集《石磴間的東西》，其實已顯示她的創作基調。除了多首觸發自生活和自然的抒情詩，比如第一首〈霜寒中剪樹〉：「**生命的彩帶在拋出的中途凍結……**」，詩集後半是一篇以中世紀民間傳說為背景，三百多行的長詩，〈愚民鎮三名智者出海以網捕月〉。她細筆描寫海上明月的變化，敘述那三人以網捕月，一切注定枉費的經過。詩人或有藉之自嘲以文字捕捉感思的徒勞。

　　2002年詩人完成第二本詩集《橡河》。這是她歷時三年的田野調查成果。整本書是一首長詩，寫那綿延七十五公里，流經英國西南部德奉郡的橡河[1]在時間流變中的故事。詩人實地探訪依河為生的擺渡人、測量員、盜捕漁夫、疏濬工、羊毛洗染工、獨木舟子、森林員等，根據這些「人」的故事，及河岸的殘骸、皮毛、頭髮、指甲等生物遺跡，描繪出一條河的生命。詩裡一切反浪漫的腐朽、衰敗、種種不堪，因為詩人抒情的筆法而得以舒緩。全書內容踏實，結構緊密，想像豐富，文字細膩，為她贏來了當年艾略特詩獎。知名文評作家珍妮・溫特生（J. Winterson）說歐思華「將荒郊野地的外境，變成慾望所在的內景」。

---

[1] 橡河（River Dart），Dart 一字字根 Dar 在凱爾特語是「橡樹」。

歐思華的詩約略有兩大類場域：大自然與古典文學。2005 年的《樹林等等》及 2009 年的《夢遊瑟芬河》與《雜草與野花》，證實了她鑽研題材與精煉文字的自我要求。《樹林等等》裡的〈聖詠致彩虹〉有這樣兩行：

> **願我常在一個字的斷橋上醒來**
> **像蛛網的痕跡在風中。無所牽繫**

《雜草與野花》獲得泰德‧休斯詩獎；但真正展現她創作高度的，應該是她 2011 年的長詩集《紀念碑》。

《紀念碑》是一篇輓歌、反戰詩。詩人帶著考古學家的冷靜態度，及匿名旁觀者肅穆的眼睛，重現荷馬史詩《伊里亞德》的特洛伊戰爭。她不寫英雄的傲人事蹟，只寫「**肩並肩，在孤獨與訝異中死去**」的不幸無名戰士與倖存家屬的哀痛。她像是從史詩的後門潛入城堡，傾聽那些在廚房或臥室避難的老弱婦孺，如何為她們橫屍沙場的父親、丈夫與兒子哭泣。

結合了政治與個人，這首詩探討的是戰爭與犧牲之無謂，以及慈悲的本質。在向史詩致敬的同時，歐思華也極有技巧地責問了荷馬的英雄崇拜和父權思維。對於歐思華，《伊里亞德》是一個豁口，從中她看見荷馬所見，再以女性視角與冷凝筆法，重新思考事件。詩集主編說這首長詩「根植於詩歌的口述傳統，帶著一種煉金術與薩滿巫術的力量」。

《紀念碑》入圍艾略特詩獎短名單。由於那一年的詩獎轉由一避險基金公司贊助，歐思華覺得與理念不合而退選；但次年，2013 年，她不負眾望拿下兩個雙年大獎：華韋克寫作獎及波普斯坵歐洲詩獎。

接下來是她 2016 年出版，再度連奪格瑞芬詩獎2 和柯斯塔詩獎3 兩個大獎的《沉沉醒來》。

《沉沉醒來》分成兩部分：前半是二十二首抒情詩，後半是一首長詩〈黎明的人〉，副題「黎明生命中的四十六分鐘」。

歐思華的繆斯是光影與水，是時間、天候、生長、腐敗與無常。她要求讀者用眼睛感覺，用觸覺聆聽，訓練讀者「換位」，去做一隻鳥，一株盆景，甚至一具屍體。例如那首〈天鵝〉，她寫一隻死去的天鵝，對著自己腐爛瓦解中的身體感嘆**怎樣一種細節的浪費／怎樣每根羽毛下的沉重」**。

〈黎明的人〉主角名叫遯叟納斯4。希臘神話中他是個吟遊詩人，也是特洛伊王子，與特洛伊國王普利阿莫同輩。有說他愛上黎明女神，也有說是黎明女神迷戀上他；不論如何，他因此成了「黎明的人」。女神為了與他長相廝守，請求宙斯賜他永生並獲得應允；但女神忘了請求宙斯也賜遯叟納斯青春永駐，遯叟納斯因此逐日衰老，終至無法行動，只能天天守著窗喃喃自語，等待黎明出現⋯⋯最後變成一隻蟋蟀，在黎明前不停嘶鳴。——據柏拉圖說，詩人死了會變成蟋蟀。

長詩寫的就是那等待黎明的詩人，從清晨 4:17 到 5:03 如夢似醒間的念頭，整首詩有音樂的時間感，也帶著貝克特短劇的實驗性。2016 年曾有《衛報》記者問歐思華是否覺得自己的詩「愈寫愈黑暗」？她說她熱愛生命的活力，但也不介意生命的剝蝕與腐敗，因為有死亡才有生命循環。

---

2 Warwick Prize for Writing 及 Popescu Prize for European Poetry。
3 Griffin Poetry Prize 及 Costa Award for Poetry。
4〈黎明的人〉英文篇名〈Tithonus〉即主角之名，遯叟納斯。Tithonus 是古希臘文 Titone（黎明女神）的陽性詞，意為「黎明女神的伴侶」。

她喜歡詩有融冰的形狀，會消失，只存在片刻。

●

2018 年歐思華與英國前輩畫家威廉‧提利爾5 攜手創作詩畫集，在畫家八十歲畫展時出版。那些詩作之後經歐思華重編、增補、修改，在 2019 年結集，成為她第八本，也是最神祕的一本詩集，《無名人》。這是繼《紀念碑》之後，歐思華再次以荷馬史詩為靈感完成的長詩集。

如果說《紀念碑》是一座陣亡將士紀念碑，見證《伊里亞德》戰爭的血腥，將烽火的烙印留在大地；《無名人》描寫的則是《奧德賽》英雄渡海返鄉的遭遇：一些流動的，斷續的，未成形的，痕跡無處可尋的故事。詩人像是藉著海洋訴說「空無」，世間一切勢必被遺忘、湮滅的命運。

詩集名「Nobody」一字的希臘文 Outis 有幾種解釋：「無人」（沒有人），「無名小卒」或「無形體的匿名者」。這書名當然讓人聯想到狄金遜名句：**我是無名小卒／你是誰？**但它其實源自《奧德賽》中一段插曲：特洛伊戰爭結束，奧德修斯在回航綺色佳途中，與屬下在塞弗洛斯島被獨眼巨怪拘禁山洞。獨眼巨怪命令奧德修斯報上姓名，奧德修斯答：「我是 Nobody」。在屬下陸續遭巨怪吞食後，奧德修斯設計以木椿刺瞎了巨怪。巨怪的慘叫引來同夥關切，卻因他一再大喊「沒有人在洞裡，沒有人刺瞎了我」而紛紛離去，奧德修斯與手下便順利脫逃。

「Nobody」這一簡單卻多義的字，也暗示了《無名人》這本詩集的撲朔迷離。長詩採多角敘事。敘事者包括返抵家門即遭妻

---

5 William Tillyer（1938-）英國當代重要畫家。

刺殺的邁錫尼國王阿加梅儂；為丈夫殺女以祭海神而懷恨，之後移情別戀的王后克呂泰涅斯特拉；與王后相戀並密謀弒君，以報殺父之仇再奪回王位的國王堂兄埃吉斯特斯；以及受國王之託監視王后，卻被放逐荒島的宮廷詩人。除此，許多希臘神話人物也如幽靈飄忽出入，比如：海神之子普洛特斯、日神海利歐斯、命運女神、奧菲斯、赫密士、殉情投海變成翠鳥的阿賽歐妮、愛上奧德修斯的海精靈卡莉普綏、想插翅飛離小島而墜海的伊卡洛斯等。敘述的語氣隨敘事者的身分而變化，起伏跌宕如多聲部複調。長詩開篇這樣寫：

……這首詩就游移在這些故事的灰色地帶。
詩的聲調被風吹散被水漬損，彷彿有個人
剛要開口吟唱《奧德賽》，卻被一艘船
帶去岩石島……

詩人描寫阿加梅儂在浴池遇刺：

命運之神割斷了他的咽喉
他就像水滴晃悠在這
　　潮汐
　　　　填滿的
　　蝕洞

在垂死掙扎中，阿加梅儂仍覺自己「並非無名小卒也許值得／比我命定的輝煌稍微光彩些的境遇……」。

詩裡形容那孤島上的宮廷詩人「乾得像菸灰缸在那兒踱步／虛構幾首拼湊不齊的關於我們的詩」。而對翅膀已經融化，往海裡快速墜落的伊卡洛斯，歐思華寫：

他的暈眩感攀升攀升
將他專注而疑惑的目光
直直帶到視野最高處他忽然就看清
他的命運已昭然揭示他撲動雙臂
　　　　驚飛
　　　幾乎樂於就此放棄
　　他開始
墜落

　　就這樣，歐思華以不聚焦的半透明筆法，帶領二十一世紀的讀者進入史詩虛實難辨的氛圍；而詩集裡那些全然空白，或只有一行文字的書頁，更開啟了我們詩的想像……

一切是如何開始的呢海的起點無止無盡

●

　　《紐約客》評論《無名人》，說歐思華戲劇化的語言彷彿海神或水銀，滑溜、多變，是大膽的實驗，像一首前衛音樂，催眠著讀者在似懂非懂中接受它，其中的距離感時時考驗讀者的「迷航忍受力」。

　　距離感，前衛，大膽的實驗。這些評論，我想，歐思華應該會欣然接受。她曾說多數人以為詩是為了撫慰人心，但對她，詩是偉大的攪亂者：「詩的本質是激進的，它質疑思維的既有秩序……可以在思想的根源起作用。」

　　2019年在「牛津詩歌教授」任上第一場演講，詩人的主題是「The Art of Erosion」，剝蝕的藝術。她說詩有兩種寫法，一種是增建法（添加），一種是剝蝕法（削減）。她的詩試圖呈現大自

然與時間的力量,其中的無常與殘缺,一種「剝蝕」的過程:剝蝕,是時間的印記,時間的藝術。

《無名人》似乎也透露出詩人無以名之的生存,或創作,的焦慮:《奧德賽》寫荒島上的英雄因自稱「無人」而得救;《無名人》裡荒島上的詩人一再狂喊「有人在嗎?有人在嗎?」卻無人回應。——回應他的,是潮浪,是烈日,是風;無人拯救他於孤獨與消失。在詩集前後,歐思華多次提到「流動」兩字:Fluid,Liquid。詩是流動的,她說。是否這部詩集,一如書封最底處那一行小字「一首海的讚美詩」所示,最終是為了讚美海,海的特質,及它所象徵的一切:神祕,不確定,流動……遺忘?

綜觀歐思華的創作,她不寫「非個人經歷」或「主題公園式」的詩。她筆下的大自然如夢似幻,卻來自清醒的現實觀察;重新詮釋的古典故事,則充滿了人道思索與無分別的不忍之心。另一特點是:她極重視詩的口述傳統,認為詩除了文字,也是聲音的雕塑。她強調朗誦之重要,以為朗讀的當下性與文字的流傳性,應該並存;因為讀詩的語調、聲音變化,會帶給詩不同的生命力。「詩是一種古老的記憶系統,需要被大聲聽到,或至少用讀樂譜的方式去讀,以激發想像的,有別於理性的,對詩的了解,」她說……

> 但這就是海
> 依然背對著我
> 千變萬化的形貌一律朝向他方
> 而誰又能解讀
> 萬籟中這一聲響
>
> 你聽

無名人
NOBODY

愛莉絲・歐思華
Alice Oswald

When Agamemnon went to Troy, he paid a poet to spy on his wife, but another man rowed the poet to a stony island and seduced her. Ten years later, Agamemnon came home and was murdered.

Odysseus, setting out at the same time, was blown off course. It took him another ten years to get home, but his wife, unlike Agamemnon's, had stayed faithful.

This poem lives in the murkiness between those stories. Its voice is wind-blown, water-damaged, as if someone set out to sing the Odyssey, but was rowed to a stony island and never discovered the poem's ending.

啟航特洛伊之前，阿加梅儂僱了一名詩人監視他的妻子，沒料到另一個男人用一艘船把那詩人送到一座岩石島，再誘拐了那人妻。阿加梅儂十年後返鄉，一進家門就命喪黃泉。

同一時間奧德修斯也啟航，被風吹離航道，又多漂泊了十年才返抵家門。和阿加梅儂不同的是，他的妻子，忠貞地，等著他。

這首詩就游移在這些故事的灰色地帶。詩的聲調被風吹散被水漬損，彷彿有個人剛要開口吟唱《奧德賽》，卻被一艘船帶去岩石島，再無法探知詩的結局。

'Also there was a poet there, whom Agamemnon, when he went to Troy, ordered strictly to guard his wife; but once Fate had forced her to be seduced, then Aegistheus took the poet to a desert island and left him there as a lump of food for the birds, so the lover willingly took her willing to his house...'

(*The Odyssey* 3 267)

啟航特洛伊之前，阿加梅儂當場交代
一名詩人監守他的妻子
但既然命運之神要那妻子出軌
埃吉斯特斯就將那詩人載到一座荒島，拋下
像一頓美食給鳥兒加餐，如此他的戀人
便滿心歡喜順勢進了他屋裡……

《奧德賽》3　267

As the mind flutters in a man who has travelled widely
and his quick-winged eyes land everywhere
I wish I was there or there he thinks and his mind

immediately

as if passing its beam through cables
flashes through all that water and lands
less than a second later on the horizon
and someone with a telescope can see his tiny thought-form
floating on the sea-surface wondering what next

那曾經四海雲遊的男人心如驚鳥
眼如飛翅隨處著陸想著
但願我是在那邊或在那邊他的意念

瞬間

像光束通過電纜
閃過整片水域和陸地短短不到
一分鐘後降落地平線
有人用望遠鏡就能看到他的思維具體而微
漂浮海面困惑著然後呢

These stories flutter about
as fast as torchlight

even out here where the water is painfully clear
and to drown in it is to sense the movement of its colour
as a cold mathematical power have you not heard
even out here these stories
how in her house of silverware and deep baths
a woman began to dream she began to wake
and the heart stirring inside her clothes felt bruised
as if a hand was squeezing it

這些故事迅如火炬
四處煽動

甚至在這兒在這水質過分清澈
沉溺其中便能感受水色流動
像冷感的數學次方難道你甚至
在這兒也沒聽到這些故事嗎那女人
如何在銀器閃閃浴池深深的屋裡
開始做夢她開始醒來
她的心在衣衫裡翻攪感覺受傷
像是一隻手正在捏擠它

She said my friend someone is watching us you will not
win over you will not walk over me easily
as over the shallows of a river but Fate
that great failure of the will that great goddess
putting on a tremulous voice and smiling
and dressed in the white bathrobe of her lover
said dearest I have already doomed that watcher
I took him to an island the merest upthrust
of a stony shoulder sticking from the sea
and he paces there as dry as an ashtray
making up poems about us patchwork unfinished
while the sea-crows traipse to and fro regarding him sideways
what does it matter what he sings
there is all this water between us
and it is blind a kind of blind blue eye
it is alive it is dead it more or less ignores us
look at all these ripples everywhere complete with their shadows
I do not think a human for example
drowning in this measureless mosaic or floating up again
I do not think he will

hear us

她說我的朋友啊有人正在監視我們
你贏不了的你沒法輕易獲得我
像輕易跨過一個淺灘但命運
那意志的摧毀者那偉大的女神
偽裝出微微顫抖的聲音帶著笑
披上她情夫的白浴袍說
最最親密的人啊那盯梢的已經被我解決了
已經被我丟棄到一座小島那小小一角
隆起的石肩凸出海面
他乾得像菸灰缸在那兒踱步
虛構幾首拼湊不齊的關於我們的詩
而海鴉無精打采來回走動乜眼瞄他
誰管他咕噥些甚麼呢
他和我們隔著漲滿的水
水是盲目的某種藍色盲眼
它是活的是死的水幾乎不理會我們
看看這四周陰影深處水波蕩漾
這麼說吧我不以為一個人
溺死或從這無垠的馬賽克再浮起來
我不以為他能

聽到我們

These voices flit about quick-winged
with women's faces or land on a clifftop singing
so that here and there you find fading contrails of song
and a swimmer slooshing along breathing in and out
with the purple sea circling his throat always
thinks he can hear something which nevertheless escapes him

貌似女性這些聲音
撲翅竄飛或哼唱著降落峭壁頂端
如此你聽到這裡那裡餘音裊繞
一個人載浮載沉氣喘吁吁游著泳
紫色海洋一圈圈環繞他的咽喉
他總以為他能聽到那終究閃躲著他的甚麼

Poor man she says poor man it's obvious
the sea in its dark psychosis dreams of your death
but your upwardness your quick turnover like a wedge of polystyrene
always keeps you afloat this place is formless and unstable
it's as long as winter nevertheless you must swim
wind yourself in my veil and the sea which always senses your fear
will fall as flat as a pressed flower you shouldn't know this
it is not me but close to me a kind of cloud or smoke-ring
made of nothing and yet it will outlast everything
because it is deep it is a dead field fenceless
a thickness with many folds in it promiscuous and mingling
which in its patience always wears away the hard things

or is it only the hours on their rounds
thinking of the tides by turns
twelve white-collar workers
who manage the schedules of water
opening and shutting the mussel shells and adjusting
from black to turquoise the swinging sea-lights
so that the sun sinking through bladderwrack
into interminable aquarium
finds even far down there are white

stones

可憐啊她說可憐的男人啊顯然這海
在思覺失調的晦暗中夢到你的死
但你的仰姿你的快速翻轉讓你像保麗龍塞子
漂浮不墜但這地方無有形狀變化多端
冗長如冬你卻必須游啊游
捲進我的帷幕而海深知你的恐懼
海會像一朵壓花扁平墜下你不該知道這些
那不是我但近似我像某種雲或煙圈
無所從來卻比一切更長久因為
它深不可測它是死寂之地沒有藩籬
一種厚度皺褶層層混亂而駁雜
永遠能以它的耐力耗蝕堅實之物

也或許那只是時間輪番迴繞
思考著潮汐
十二個白領工人
掌管水的日程表
把蚌殼開開關關
把海搖晃的光色由漆黑調成青藍
讓落日穿過墨角藻
進入無止盡的水族世界
發現那最底最深處竟然也是白色的

岩石

And suddenly in the violet dark
a bronze fish-hook flickers into life and out again

and when it rains and the sand has every ounce of me
marked at low tide and immediately forgotten
so that my footprints far into the future
go on sunkenly walking underneath me
when it rains it snows sometimes
as if falling asleep the body began to float

sideways

而暗紫之中驟然
一枚青銅魚鉤一閃刺入生命再從中拔起

當雨來了泥沙占據我每一寸肌膚
留下退潮的印記又即刻遺忘
如此我那步入遙遠未來的腳印
便一步步沉陷到我下方
雨來了有時雪來了
彷彿陷入夢境軀體開始漂向

側方

There are so many birds and most of them mean nothing
but once or twice a gannet
from a nest of slovenly seaweed
                        hops
as far as those stones and stops
as a woman would remembering her son

but it is done madam nothing will close that wound
unless your shaken mind moving your pointed head
can stitch the water to the wind
or is it only her ghost going round and round
with a remnant of blue
and never a clue where to place it
or is it only that poet pacing to and fro
dreaming up rumours about the first kiss
buzzing on those lovers' flypaper lips

到處是鳥但多數一無意義
除了偶爾一隻塘鵝
從散漫的海藻窩
　　　　　一竄
竄上最遠能及的石堆又停下
像個女人回想起她的愛兒

但事已至此夫人啊傷口再無法癒合
除非妳撼動的意志能驅使妳敏銳的頭腦
將水與風彌縫
或是否這只是她的幽魂圈圈盤旋
帶著殘留的一縷藍
永遠不知該安置何處
或是否這只是那詩人來回踱步
幻想些關於那初吻的謠傳
在戀人們捕蠅紙的唇邊嗡嗡作聲

Small geometric figure
lost inside colour

he keeps wading out then back but it is
bottomless dusk down there pale black
nameless and numbness as when unfolding after sleeping
and your own dead foot has forgotten you
as if I waded inward
thirty yards from the surface of myself
but it's not myself it's just dark purple
it's not my feet it is the hours that move

if only the birds had subtitles if only by staring
I could draw some of those directions into my mind

小小的幾何形體
消失在色彩中

他一次次涉水往外走又回到原地
下方是無底的陰影灰敗的黑
無名且無感彷彿入睡後舒展開
黃泉路上你的腳步已不記得你
彷彿我從自己表層往內
涉行三十碼
但那不是我是一片黑紫
那移動的不是我的腳是時間

多麼希望群鳥能提供字幕多麼希望
只盯著看我就能在腦海畫下一二方位

And sometimes over my retina
as over an angled mirror an aeroplane
sometimes between two clouds with wingtips
teetering on the very pivot of vision a passenger
throws down her shadow
in which I catch the tiny movement of her eye-blinds

lifting

and in this cloud/uncloud I who can't settle
when I think of that crowd of colours on the sea
then my mind starts sliding towards them
borne on a wave of wind

有時掠過我視網膜
像掠過斜角鏡一架飛行器
有時在兩朵雲之間以翼尖
搖擺在視線正中央一個過客
拋下她的陰影
陰影裡我捕捉到她一個小動作把眼罩

掀開

在雲開雲闔間我心神不定
想到海面紛湧的色彩
我的思緒便隨著風的波浪
滑向它們

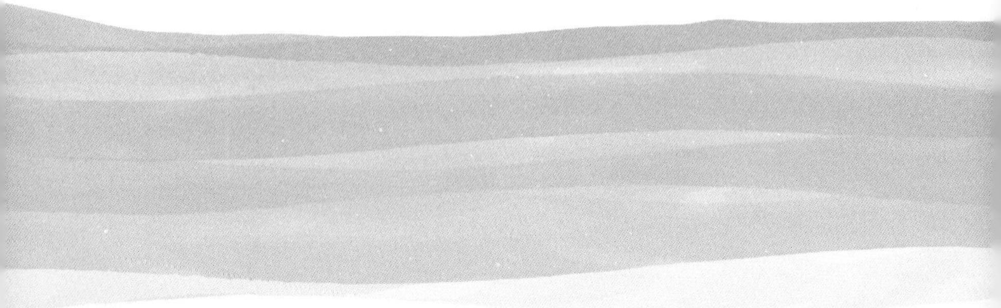

As far as a man can shout across water
and his shout with blown-back wings
loses its bearings and is never heard of again
and another man can hear the crying waves
but his answer
dissolves in water like an oval of soap

they say this woman being twisted by sleep
began to hear things
as if the sea itself leaned over her bed
she could hear they say the exact note
in which a diver twizzles like a mobile
among triangular hanged fish
and the sea wall and the weakening cliffs
as far as the hem of her clothes

                    being eaten away

一個男人在隔海極遠處呼叫
他的呼叫聲反剪著翅膀
失去方向再也不復聽見
另一個男人聽見波浪哭號
但他的答覆
溶解在水中一如肥皂的橢圓形狀

他們說這女人被睡夢糾纏
開始幻聽
彷彿海俯身在她床邊
她能清楚聽到每一個字他們說
有個潛海人像床頭吊飾般
在垂掛的三角形魚群及
海牆與趨緩的峭壁間旋轉
直到杳遠杳遠她的衣褙

　　　　被吞噬之處

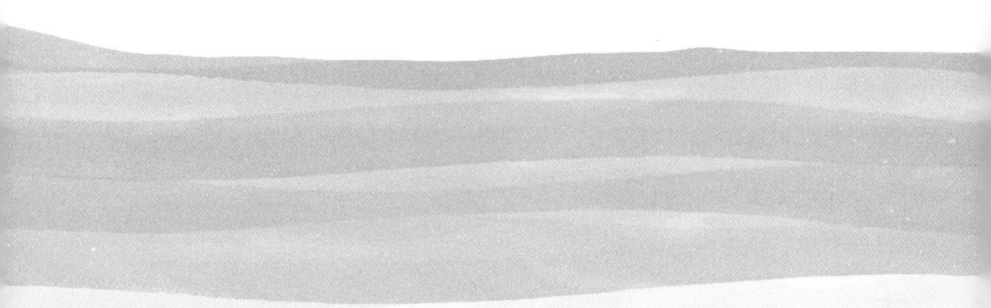

How does it start the sea has endless beginnings

一切是如何開始的呢海的起點無止無盡

About an hour ago she surfaced and shook her arms
and peered around and dived again and surfaced
and saw someone and dived again and surfaced
and smelt all those longings of grass-flower smells
and bird-flower sounds and the vaporous poems
that hang in the chills above rivers

一個鐘頭前她從水底浮起揮舞雙臂
環顧四方又潛入又浮起
看見有人又再潛入再浮起
嗅聞著種種渴望那花草的氣息
花鳥的鳴叫那氤氳的詩
冷冷懸在河上

With crooked elbows walking and small steps
she hops to these hollow limestone caves
where the seals breathing out the sea's bad breath
snuffle about all afternoon in sleeping bags
what kind of a rumour is beginning even now
under the waterlid she wonders there must be
hundreds of these broken and dropped-open mouths
sulking and full of silt on the seabed
I know a snorkeller found a bronze warrior once
with the oddest verdigris expression and maybe
even now a stranger is setting out
onto this disintegrating certainty this water
whatever it is whatever anything is
under these veils and veils of vision
which the light cuts but it remains

unbroken

手肘扭曲變形踩著小步子
她蹬進凹陷的石灰岩洞
洞裡幾隻海豹吐出海的穢氣
一整個下午在睡袋裡抽著鼻子
這時候水面下還能散播出甚麼
謠傳呢她想這海床上
該有上百張碎嘴子大開著
滿口泥沙悶悶不樂
我知道有個潛水人曾經找到一個青銅戰士
帶著極其古怪的銅鏽表情而或許
就在這當下有個陌生人正出發
前來這崩解中的未知來到這水域
不管是甚麼不管是任何甚麼
在這被光線切割的層層
視覺帷幕下它依然

完整

So we floated out of sight into the unmarked air
and only our voices survived
like thistle-seed flying this way and that

a blue came over us a blue cloud
whose brown shadow goose-fleshed the sea
the ship after a little rush stopped moving
the wind with a swivelling sound began to rise
and here I am still divided in my decision
whether to heave-to or keep going under half-sail
but the water is in my thinking now
I remember the mast-pole broken by a gust
severed my two minds separate
and my body flopped like a diver over the side
then came the invisible then the visible rain
then icy and razor-sharp then green then dawn
who always wakes behind net curtains
and her watercolour character changes shade quickly like new leaves
she is excitable then shy then coppery pink
and raking her fingers around finds bits of clothing and bones

如此我們飄出視線進入茫茫虛空
只有我們的聲音倖存
如薊草籽四處飄飛

一抹藍向我們襲來一朵憂鬱的雲
褐色的陰影讓海冒出雞皮疙瘩
小船疾駛片刻便不再動彈
風隨氣旋聲往上攀升
而我仍舉棋不定
不知該停航或減速持續前行
但如今我會顧忌到水了
想到那船桅遭狂風摧折
斷裂了我二分的意念分歧
身體像潛水人側翻落水
然後雨來了忽隱忽顯
然後冷如冰利如刃然後一片綠然後
黎明永遠在網簾背面甦醒
她水彩般的個性彷彿新葉瞬間變色
她容易興奮又害羞化為銅粉紅
手指四處耙搜著找到些破衣服碎骨頭

How strange she says among those better worlds underwater
where the cold of swimming is no different from the clear of looking
there are people still going about their work
unfurling sails and loosening knots
it's as if they didn't know they were drowned
it's as if I blinded by my own surface
have to keep moving over seemingly endless yellowness
have to keep moving over seemingly endless yellowness

多奇怪啊她說在那更完美的水底世界
汹水之冷與觀看之透徹成等比
仍然有人繼續工作
張開船帆鬆開繩結
彷彿不知己身已溺死
彷彿我蒙昧於自己的表相
必須保持動作超越那彷彿無盡的昏黃
必須保持動作超越那彷彿無盡的昏黃

How does the dawn trawler call out to the night trawler
when they pass each other on the black and white water

黎明的網漁人如何招喚黑夜的網漁人
當他們擦肩而過在黑水白水之上

There are said to be microscopic insects in the eye
who speak Greek and these invisible
ambassadors of vision never see themselves
but fly at flat surfaces and back again
with pigment caught in their shivering hair-like receptors
and this is how the weather gets taken to and fro
and the waves pass each other from one colour to the next
and sometimes mist a kind of stupefied rain
slumps over the water like a teenager
and sometimes the sun returns whose gold death mask
with its metallic stare seems to be

blinking

據說眼睛裡有一群能說希臘語的
微型昆蟲這些無形的
視覺大使從來看不見自己
卻飛行在平滑表面攜回牠們
以顫動的纖毛狀接收器攫獲的顏料
氣候因此得以來去往返
而潮浪競逐色彩一波超越另一波
有時霧是呆滯的雨
像一個少年栽進水裡
有時太陽回頭它金色的死亡面具
那金屬質的凝視似乎

眨了一下

Two fishermen rowing across saw something jagged and disturbing
the long-drawn-out Now of a teenager
pale green and full of unripe hope
he had dressed himself in wings this is exciting
I like the angle of attack when these graded feathers
glued in their waxy grooves begin to swim the air

winding his giddiness up and up
carrying his steadfast sceptical stare
right to the summit of sight he noticed suddenly
his fate had been found out and flapping his arms

        flushed

      and almost glad to give up

    he began to

fall

兩名漁夫划船經過看到讓人不安的畸形物
那是一個慘綠少年無盡延長的當下
充滿未成熟的願望
他為自己裝上翅膀那簡直太酷了
我愛那撞擊的角度當那一根根黏在蠟槽
排列有序的羽毛開始在半空游泳

他的暈眩感攀升攀升
將他專注而疑惑的目光
直直帶到視野最高處他忽然就看清
他的命運已昭然若揭他撲動雙臂

    驚飛

   幾乎樂於就此放棄

  他開始

墜落

What a relief to hear his flesh
with hair and clothes flaring backwards like a last-minute flower
hit the sea and finally understand itself
his human-salt already at ease in the ocean-salt
and the white silt-like substance of exhaustion
blending with the water

    if only

if only my eyes could sink under the surface
and join those mackerel shoals in their matching suits
whose shivering inner selves all inter-mirrored
all in agreement with water
wear the same

wings

令人寬慰的是聽說他的肉身
像臨終的花頭髮衣裳往後飄飛
栽進海裡而終究明白
他體內的鹽分已經自在地溶入海鹽
而那白色泥沙般的殘餘物質
正混融於水

  多麼希望

多麼希望我的眼睛能沉入水底
加入那群外觀相同的鯖魚
牠們顫慄的內在自我全然相互映照
全然與水契合
有相同的

  鰭翼

But this is the sea
still with its back to me
in its flesh of a thousand faces all facing away
and who can decipher this
voice among voices

    listen

但這就是海
依然背對著我
千變萬化的面貌一律朝向他方
而誰又能解讀
萬籟中這一聲響

  你聽

This is one kind of water when it hangs over him
a man is a nobody underneath a big wave
his loneliness expands his hair floats out like seaweed
and when he surfaces his head full of green water
sitting alone on his raft in the middle of death
then it is wide it is a wide field of horrible upheavals
there are fish in it there are shearwaters searching
and sometimes in these gulfs a goddess
who used to be human now she is yellow-eyed
sometimes she shrieks heavy-winged with laughterless laughter
and lands on his raft shaking the underworld off
poor man she says poor man it's obvious
you can sniff it everywhere the shabby weirdness
of the sea-god leaning intimately over
and turning his shadows against you
poor morsel of cork you bob about
throwaway in all this what is it grief grief grief
but this grief is so old its matter has lost its mind
blinks blinks and sees nothing
howls howls and hears nothing

是這樣一種水高懸在他上方
巨浪下一個男人無名無姓
他的寂寞擴張他的頭髮如海藻漂散
當他浮現時他的顱內灌滿綠水
孤零零坐在筏上在死亡的中途
然後是寬闊極其寬闊可怖的騷亂地帶
其中有魚有搜掠的鷗鳥
有時海溝出現一位女神
她原先是人現在有火眼金睛
有時尖聲怪叫兩翼沉重似笑非笑
從冥府脫身降落他的筏上
可憐啊她說可憐的男人啊顯然
你處處嗅得到那邋遢
又古怪的海神俯身貼近
將陰影投向你
可悲的一截軟木塞啊你隨波逐流
漂泊其中這到底是甚麼呢悲哀啊悲哀
但這悲哀太古老它只餘物質無有心智
眨眼再眨眼甚麼也看不見
喊叫又喊叫甚麼也聽不到

And yet again water still in acute discomfort

always yearning and hallucinating and dedicated to the wind
and yet again the wind not fully awake
or was it laughter blew me along I lost track of
the underneath of things everything became my mirror
once I stood up to look over the side
I sat down again terrified it was myself I saw
thronged and pitch-green
spilling over the lip of the earth
the same soft dust-sheets over my hands as the clouds
the same thick curtain across the horizon as
sheer boredom and a deep

    sea-breath

而水依然騷動不已

永遠渴望著幻想著為風獻身
而風依然半夢半醒
或是否那嘯笑聲吹颭著我而我失去了
事情的線索一切都成了我的鏡子
有一回我起身側望
又悚然坐下發現我看見的是自己看見
一大片瀝青綠
溢出大地的唇邊
同樣柔軟的防塵布覆蓋我雙手彷彿雲
同樣厚重的帷幕橫過地平線彷彿
純粹的厭倦以及沉沉的

　　　海的呼吸

In which a spirit leaning languorously from a porthole
poured stillness over the sea like a jug of milk
and there were bones everywhere and feathered people
stood singing on the stones on rickety thin legs
with tilted chins and pressed flat wings

其中有個幽靈懶散傾斜著從崗哨口
把死寂往海裡倒像是倒牛奶
到處都是殘骸全身羽毛的人
支著細腿搖晃晃站在岩石上吟唱
下巴翹起翅膀壓低

If you should see they said if you could spare
a moment to make out if you have any heart
to hear us mourn in short syllables
now that the stillness is pale blue
and apparitions of islands like pre-world humans
are waiting to evolve but always before they can grow detail
the air aborts them and the clouds
bafflingly quiet as if the fact of floating
had taken some weight off their minds
the clouds pause like holy men
very close and far-off in their white shrouds of office

他們說如果你剛巧看到如果你能挪出
一分鐘辨認如果你有一絲同情
聆聽我們短音節的哀悼
此刻死寂已化為灰藍
島嶼的幽靈如史前人類
等待著演化但永遠在長出細部之前
又化入空氣而雲
安靜得惱人彷彿飄浮這事實
已帶走他們心智的一些份量
雲且停步彷彿聖人
穿著白色法衣在咫尺天涯

If you should see a pair of blinking eyes
blue and red with weeping no sooner seen than gone
you should know they are kingfishers
man and wife in these amazing clothes
who lay their eggs on fish-bones
and for nine days when they nest the wind drops
and the hooded waves remembering their story
stammer to a hush they used to be humans

whose flesh stalks always true to the light
were on the point of flowering but the sea
which has no faith no patience
just kleptomaniac and fickle currents

drowned him

如果你剛巧看到一雙淚眼眨啊眨
泛紅泛藍瞬間出現又消失
你知道那是翠鳥
衣著鮮亮一夫一妻
他們在魚骸上產卵
九天孵卵期間風速降緩
罩著兜帽的海浪記得他們的故事
結巴著安靜下來他們曾經是人

肉莖性喜向陽
花期幾乎可待但海
沒有信心沒有耐性
只有竊盜癖和善變的浪

溺死了他

It was horrible when the rising sun
wrinkled her skin as it worked its way in
and the widow at the window saw at once
her bloated husband's head oh pray for the crowded
ragged dead in the crypts of the sea
where the boneless octopus
        only exists by endlessly altering
pray for the hollowed out souls
in the skins of the living whose lifted clothes

        became

                birds

恐怖的是當太陽升起
闖進屋裡弄皺了她的皮膚
那站在窗邊的寡婦立即看到她膨脹的
夫婿那顆頭顱噢為那些支離破碎
堆擠在海底地窖的亡者祈禱吧
在那裡無骨的章魚
只憑不斷變形存活
為那些靈魂被掏空的活死人
祈禱吧他們掀起的衣衫

　　已化成

　　　飛鳥

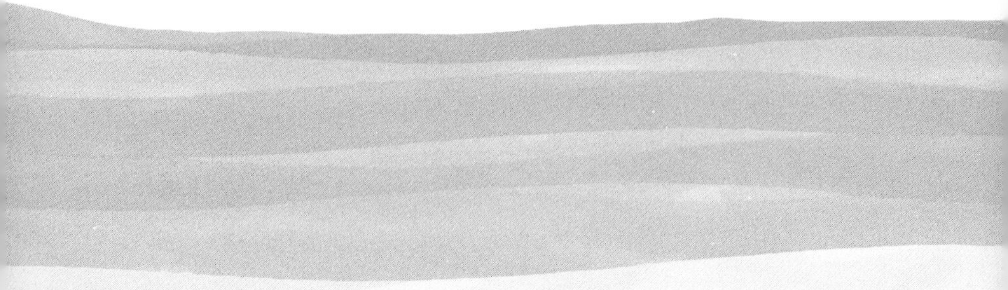

When trees take over an island and say so all at once
some in pigeon some in pollen with a coniferous hiss
and run to the shore shouting for more light
and the sun drops its soft coverlet over their heads
and owls and hawks and long-beaked sea-crows
flash to and fro
like spirits of sight whose work is on the water
where the massless mind undulates the intervening air
shading it blue and thinking

       I wish I was there

or there

樹一旦占領島嶼且立即宣示主權
有些便跟隨鴿子有些憑藉花粉帶著
針葉樹的嘶喊奔向海岸索討更多陽光
太陽便拋下柔軟的被單罩在它們頭頂
夜梟和老鷹和長喙海鴉
穿梭閃現
彷彿視覺的精靈在水面工作
那兒無質量的心念晃動
把介入其間的空氣藍染且想著

   但願我是在那邊

或那邊

A goddess or fog-shape in full wedding dress
sulks in that loneliness what a winter creature
whose lover loathes the everlasting clouds of her
and sits in tears staring at the pleasure-crinkled sea
but she as if a dash of hope
discoloured her sight stands waiting
the way a spider when it wishes to travel
simply lets out a silken

      aerial

electrostatically alert through every hair
to the least shift of the ionosphere
at last it lifts on tiptoe and lovely to behold
like a bare twig it begins to blow
wherever the wind will take it but the wind
is the most distracted messenger I know

一團霧或是一個女神身穿嫁紗
在孤獨中抑鬱不樂這冬季的生物啊
她的戀人眼中有淚坐望海的笑紋
為她長久不散的烏雲懊惱
但彷彿一絲希望改變了她
視覺的色彩她起身等待
像隻渴望旅行的蜘蛛
單純地伸出一根絲質

   天線

透過每根毛髮發出靜電般的訊息
傳到離電層極遠處
然後提起腳尖優雅地
彷彿裸露的細枝子開始飄
隨風之所之
但風是最不專心的信差我知道

Whereupon the water turned in its cloak
and shook itself into flames and burnt itself into fur
and tore itself into flesh and told everything
and instantly shrank into polythene
and withered and bloomed and resolved to be less faltering

                    and failed

and became a jellyfish a mere weakness of water
a morsel of ice a glamour of oil
and became a fish-smell and then a rotting seal
and then an old mottled man full of mood-swings
forgetting his name and twisting his hands
denying and distorting and thinking ill of everything
he snapped himself into sticks and burst into leaves
which fell back down again as water
blue-green and black-shine with white lining
and blinked himself into thousands of self-seeing eyes
like a piece of writhing paper in five seconds of fire
destroying its light with its

light

於是水在披風裡一旋身
將自己揮舞成火焰焚燒成毛髮
撕裂成血肉坦白了一切
又瞬間皺縮成聚乙烯塑料
而枯萎而盛開而決心不多猶豫

    而失敗了

變成海蜇一種水的軟弱
或一小塊冰一種油脂的魅態
變成魚腥或腐敗的海豹味
變成渾身黑斑情緒不穩的老頭
忘了自己的姓名搓著雙手
對一切曲解否認不滿
他把自己折斷成枝拋散成葉
再一次墜落如水
藍綠且烏亮襯著白底
眼睛一眨把自己化作千眼反觀自身
像一張紙在短短五秒的火苗中扭動
以自身的光毀滅自身

  的光

And so the sun brought measurement to everything
all but the sea frightened of its own stupidity
and on every cliffside luminous lilies
made their escape through stones
whose swinging stems
were merely the lowest ruffling hems of the passing of spring
and above them flying in verse

in time with
the wind

於是太陽就為一切帶來節奏
除了海萬物都為自身的魯鈍而忐忑
峭壁邊鮮亮的百合
從岩石遁逃
它們搖晃的花梗不過是
春神離去時低垂的裙襬拂過
而在它們上方飄飛成韻的

與風
節拍若符

Two sisters in shock
one couldn't speak one couldn't stop
she knocked on the bedroom window

sister
        hello

what with tutting and whistling
she shoved her way in through the door
well sister if they cut out your tongue
you'll have to thread this needle and stitch me the facts
and as she stitched and stitched those sordid facts
broke through her feathered smile and became a beak

兩姊妹在驚恐中
一個瘖啞無言一個喋喋不休
她敲著臥室窗戶

妹妹
　　　妹妹啊

隨著一陣手舞足蹈啁啾嘰喳
她破門而入
好吧妹妹如果他們割了妳的舌頭
妳就為我把真相一針一線織出來
她織著織著那樁醜行
就從她羽毛掩飾的笑容迸裂變成利喙

As when the moon shines through tent walls
making black-and-white films of the woods
so that the sleepers seem to float through trees
so those two sisters
out through their back-lit flesh they fly
into the blue of amnesia

snapping at insects and can't think why

月光沁透帳篷帷幕
把森林變成黑白影片
如此睡夢中的人彷彿飄過叢樹
如此那兩姊妹
穿越她們背光的肉體
飛入遺忘之藍

撲捉著蚍蟲卻不明所以

Terrified of insects of noon of sunlight
when the sea dilates to let more green in
and the damaged undermost in all its clefts can be seen
when swallows free themselves of their sorrows
and seagulls hang themselves on invisible armatures
and only a few tiny almost magical flashes of light
fall in the form of rain and

stop

those lovers lurk in their indoors wondering
can he hear us now that poet has he finished
his poem about us what kind of a sting in the ending
will he sing of the husband if he is in fact
on his way here knowing by now the craggy out-jut
of that shallow place where the seals bob about like footballs
and did you hear along the shore that chorus of trees
with seaweed hung from their twigs like wept-in tissue
being moved by what a heartfelt sigh the wind is
and have you noticed the way the radius of water
maintains itself in proportion to its circles
as if each raindrip made a momentary calculation
and when it stops there are ruled flat lines
running from one island metrically to another

畏懼蜚蟲畏懼正午畏懼陽光
當海膨脹容許更多綠色滲入
它所有裂縫裡最底層的創傷便展露無遺
當燕子釋放了自己不再悲愴
海鷗懸空在隱形盔甲之上
而僅有些許幾乎魔幻的微弱閃光
以雨的形狀墜落

停頓

戀人們在屋內窺伺揣測著
那個詩人這時還能聽見我們嗎那首
關於我們的詩他寫好了嗎他會如何
吟唱那丈夫最終遇刺之禍呢是否
他正在途中這時已知道那淺灘區
險峻的岬角有海豹跳動如足球
而你聽見沿岸樹林的大合唱了嗎
風的嘆息流露真情讓樹枝上垂掛的
海藻像淚濕的紙巾
你注意到水
維持半徑與圓弧固定比例的方式了嗎
每滴雨彷彿都做好瞬間計算
雨一停一條條筆直的心律停止線
就從一座島嶼有韻律地奔向另一座

How does it start the sea has endless beginnings

一切是如何開始的呢海的起點無止無盡

There is a harbour where an old sea-god sometimes surfaces
two cliffs keep out the wind you need no anchor
the water in fascinated horror holds your boat
at the far end a thin-leaved olive casts a kind of evening over a cave
which is water's house where it leads its double life
there are four stone bowls and four stone jars
and the bees of their own accord leave honey there
salt-shapes hang from the roof like giant looms
where the tide weaves leathery sea-nets
be amazed by that colour it is the mind's inmost madness
but the sea itself has no character just this horrible thirst
goes on creeping over the stones and shrinking away

有一名老海神偶爾浮現在港口
港邊的峭壁能擋住風船隻無須定錨
海水在迷亂中托住你的船
遠處一株稀疏的橄欖樹用另類的夜晚蓋住蝕洞
這是水的屋宇在此它過著雙重生活
屋裡四個石碗四個石甕
蜜蜂有默契地在那兒留下蜂蜜
鹽狀結晶體自屋頂垂下彷彿巨型織布機
潮水以它織出皮革質感的海網
且為那顏色驚嘆吧那是意識最底層的瘋狂
但海本身沒有個性除了這可怕的渴
不斷悄悄爬上巖石又退縮離開

The sea she said and who could ever drain it dry
has so much purple in its caves the wind at dusk
incriminates the waves
and certain fish conceal it in their shells
at ear-pressure depth
where the shimmer of headache dwells
and the brain goes

      dark

          purple

              who could offend the sea there is so much water
we might as well waste this ever-replenished
fairy-tale stuff don't flinch she said
I want you to walk this carpet

          please oh please

you must be so so
footsore after your ten-year war you surely
deserve a little something if you
take off your shoes the bare floor will be so cold so
filthily infectious you should step down safely

here

這海她說又有誰能讓它乾涸呢
它的蝕洞裡太多紫色
風在薄暮作浪
有些貝類將它藏入甲殼
在耳壓臨界處
頭痛的微光乍閃
腦子陷入

  暗
   紫

   誰又能冒犯海呢海水實在太多了
不妨我們就別理會這沒完沒了的
傳說吧她說你別卻步
我要你走上這地毯

   請你噢請你

你的腳必定非常
痠痛經歷這十年戰火
你理該得到一些禮遇如果你
脫下鞋這光禿的地板將是多麼冷多麼
骯髒帶菌你該安全地走下來就從

這兒

That man is doomed that very second
the swelling blood-shade shows through his skin
even as he bashfully sets his foot down saying
after all I'm not nobody maybe I deserve a little
brighter something than my allotted brightness
no superstition has ever hurt an honest man perhaps
after my bath in my towel I can walk it

again

血光擴散穿透他皮膚那一霎
他已注定在劫難逃
就算他單腳怯怯落地時說
畢竟我並非無名小卒也許值得
比我命定的輝煌稍微光彩些的境遇
迷信無損誠信之人或許
沐浴完披上浴巾我又能

走了

Inside his lifted foot in its falling pause
Fate feeds on this weakness and the same
massive simplicity cuts through his throat
as drips and sways in all these

      tide

           filled

         caves

the same iridescent swiftness and the same
uncertain certainty either brimming or rippled
or swelling over of hollowing water
as one thought leads to another if you stand
here on these boulders with your back to the earth
you can see the whole story of the weather
the way the wind brings one shadow after another
but another one always sweeps up behind
and no-one can decipher this lucid short-lived
chorus of waves it is too odd and even
as if trying to remember some perfect prehistoric
pattern of spirals it is too factual too counter-factual
too copper-blue too irregular-metrical

listen

利用他舉腳落腳停頓中的
弱點與同樣巨大的無知
命運之神割斷他的咽喉吞噬了
他就像水滴晃悠在這

   潮汐

      填滿的

     蝕洞

以同樣虹彩般的速度同樣
不確定的確定或要溢出或起波紋
或膨脹於掏空的水上
就像一念引發下一念如果你站在
岩石堆上背對大地
你就能看清這天候的來龍去脈
如何風帶來重重陰影
而永遠另一陰影隨之掃過
沒有人能解析這透明而短暫的
波浪大合唱它太怪異甚至
像是試著記住一些完美的史前
漩渦圖案它太據實太反事實
太青銅藍太格律不規律

你聽

Let me tell you what the sea does
to those who live by it first it shrinks then it
hardens and simplifies and half-buries us
and sometimes you find us shivering in museums
with tilted feet so that all we can do is lie flat
our colourful suffering faces watered away
we who threw fish-lines into these waves
and steadied our weight in mastless longboats
and breathed in and out the very winds that wrecked us

讓我告訴你海對那些
討海人做了些甚麼它收縮
它硬化又單一化再半埋了我們
有時你看到我們在博物館裡顫抖
雙腳歪斜只能躺平
彩妝的痛苦的臉被水洗掉
我們這群把釣魚線拋進波浪的人
在無桅長船上穩住重心
呼吸著那置我們於劫難的風

And there are herons there are sea-ravens
whose wingspan is a whole awning
they could lift a man's flesh off its framework
and cormorants like eroded crows
and angled ospreys and harpies
all kinds of long-beaked hungers
peer from the trees and any minute now
with smashing of wings and probing of steel-grey pins
they'll come for these eyes oh horrible

    flightless

light

還有蒼鷺還有海渡鴉
牠們張開的兩翼龐大如船篷
輕易就能拆散人的皮肉和骨架子
還有鸕鶿活像風化的烏鴉
還有鉤吻魚鷹人面妖鷲
各類長喙的掠食者
在樹上隨時伺機帶著牠們
重量級翅膀和鋼鐵灰的針爪
對準這雙眼而來啊恐怖的

      不飛的

光

I've always loved the way when night happens
the blood is drawn off is sucked and soaked upwards
out of the cliff-flowers the way they worn out
surrender their colours and close and then the sky
suffers their insights all the shades of mauve green blue
move edgelessly from west to east the cold
comes ghostly out of holes and the earth it's strange
as soon as she shuts her sky-lids her hindsights open
and you can see right out through her blindness
as far as the ancient stars still making their precise points
still exactly visible and then not exactly

well there was and there was not a drowned woman
still visible underwater crossing a field
there she walks nothing can shift that moment
lodged in her chest when she was kidnapped
and her outline stayed there forever but she
now with no character only this salty bitterness
became a slave she who had rich parents
began to smell of anger sinking towards unendurable laughter
which overruns its circle like the sea itself
on whose blind glare
a boat appears full of rat-eyed sailors
squinting from watching too much sea-film

我總是著迷於如何傍晚時分
峭壁上花兒的血被抽乾
潤澤著天空如何花兒們筋疲力盡
放棄了色彩且收攏而天空
領受了花的感悟深深淺淺的藍綠粉紫
無邊無際自西徂東遷移
寒氣如幽靈從洞穴出現神奇的是
大地一旦闔起她虛空的眼瞼就有了
後見之明而你就能透過她的盲目看見
只要那遠古的星宿依然維持精準方位
依然確實可見卻不十分確實

是啊水底仍然若有似無隱約
可見一名溺水女子正越過一片原野
她一路走著無法改變無法
忘懷她被劫持的那一瞬
而她的輪廓便永久停留在那兒
但出身世家的她這時已然失去個性
只剩下淪為禁臠的苦澀
她開始渾身散發怨氣陷入難忍的狂笑
笑聲像海一圈圈擴散
在她茫然的注視下
一艘船緩緩浮現整船鼠目的水手
眼睛斜瞇著因為看多了海的軟片

Image after image it never ends
it has the texture of plough but with no harvest
but every so often a flower of light floats past
and one of them slept with her which is a woman's weakness
we must keep it she said hidden under eyelids
put lampshades on this eagerness if we meet
at the fountain for example washing our clothes or drinking
but after a while he grew bored of this patience
he came to her door with necklaces
she had a needle in her hand she looked up sharp
and her mind slipped like snow off a leaf
but the gods know everything they sent a virus
fluttering after the ship and seven days later
she dropped like a dead bird into the bilge
four sailors had to swing her over the side and the water
with all its claws and eaters closed over her
the splash became a series of dots and
under that sound the green sea turned

    grey

影像接著影像沒有止盡
像是徒勞的耕耘沒有收成
但偶爾會有一朵鮮亮的花漂過
而其中之一睡了她這是女人的弱點
我們得把祕密藏在眼底她說
為這激情加個燈罩如果我們比方說
在泉水邊洗衣或喝水時遇到
但沒多久他就按捺不住了
捧著項鍊來到她門前
她手拿織針警覺地望向天空
心思如雪滑落樹葉
但一切瞞不過諸神祂們差遣病毒
尾隨船隻整整七天後
像一隻猝死的鳥她墜落底艙
四名水手合力把她拋下大海而海
以全部的螯爪和饕客欺近她
浪花變成無數句點
砰然一聲巨響那青綠的海變色成

  灰

Transparent wisps of things with eye-like organs
sink to the seabed in shells of extraordinary beauty
and at sunset the smells float out orange
and settle on the flowers' tongues while sea-whips
thrash thrash the water for a living
nobody cares whether there is weeping or oozing
or the flavour of dead flesh fills the evening
and when the wind shifts you can hear a man
shouting for help
      cursing his wounded foot but
      nobody answers

一群透明微形物長著眼睛般的器官
隨著華麗的甲殼沉到海底
日落時橙橘飄散的氣息
停頓在花的舌尖而軟珊瑚鞭
為了生存唰唰抽打著水
沒人在意誰正流著淚或淌著血
或腐屍味充斥著夜晚
當風向驟變你可以聽到一名男子
狂喊呼救
   詛咒他負傷的腳而
   無人回應

Only night-birds eating insects
whirring and dialling in the small hours
expressing no emotion only existence
always laughing and screaming the same fact
stacked on every twig not every sound
is a voice not every breath is a self
but anything
knocked by a sudden blow
has the same unspecified shrillness oh I
feel like a glued fly giving up and standing up and
time and again stuck in the same pain if only
my foot could move my thought
and think of a cure but my thoughts can't
lift their wings and every struggle
tangles me lower I wish I was

    there or

               there

只有捕食昆蟲的夜鳥們
在凌晨時分繞圈盤旋
不表達情緒只表現存在
總對著旁枝末節上堆疊的同一件事實
狂笑尖叫但未必每一種聲響
都是人聲每一口呼吸都是主動
任何物體
受到猛然重擊
都會發出同樣無法辨識的刺耳聲啊我感覺
像是隻蒼蠅被黏住腳絕望了又站起來
一次次困於同樣的痛苦
多希望我的腳能牽動思緒
想出一個解方但我的思緒無法
舉翅高飛而每一回掙扎
都糾纏得我陷入更深但願我是在

那邊或

那邊

Misfortune I wish I could meet you
underwater in your deep green room
and flannel your bloodshot eyes
and brush your dead hair
they say there is a flash of mercy
concealed in your face-folds
if only a person has time to swim down
and find it

there are soft chairs no windows
no noise except the self-closing stone door
which I opened once
and found myself in a chamber of options
a little sea-cleft where the salmon drift
and turn into humans

but Fate is not Fortune
I was not fated to find you there
only the converging walls

        the tilted
        floor

厄運啊但願我能在水底
在你深綠的屋裡遇到你
用法蘭絨覆蓋你充血的眼睛
梳理你枯死的頭髮
他們說你的法令紋裡藏著
瞬間的悲憫
只等有人有空潛下水
找到它

屋裡有幾把軟椅沒有窗
沒有雜音除了自動關閉的石門
我曾打開那扇門
發現自己置身一間充滿各式選項的密室
一條狹小的海溝有鮭魚漂著漂著
變成人

但命運之神不是幸運之神
我命定無法在那邊找到你
只找到牆的死角

   傾斜的
   地板

And once a fisherman poking among the mackerel
pulled out a human head whose head
tell me muse about this floating nobody
the one who would have drowned but a river
coming looking for him with swerves
and trailing beard-hair how secretive it is
when water moves through the sea
keeping its muddiness intact and fish commuters
hurry under him as if motioning him in
this river touched his hand who is it
honourable river-god is it you he said
o cold tap cold mouth pick up this message o help me
I come to you upside-down with empty suckers
crawling along the sea surface on my knees
stripped of everything even gravity have mercy

曾經有個漁夫翻攪一堆鯖魚時
撈出一顆人頭這是誰的頭呢
繆斯啊跟我說說這無名氏漂浮的故事吧
這人該早已溺死但一條河
帶著蜿蜒拖曳的髮鬃
前來找他多麼神祕啊
當水流經大海
保持一貫的渾濁而魚群在他下方
往來匆匆彷彿推動著他
在這河裡觸摸他的手是誰呢
高貴的河神啊是祢嗎他說
啊冷冷的拍打冷冷的嘴撿起這訊息吧救救我
我倒栽著來找祢帶著空空的吸盤
在海面匍匐膝行
我已失去一切甚至失去了重力請憐憫我

Tell me muse about this ancient passer-by
who found himself adrift in infinite space
with all the planets flying in loops around him
like listless gods
all kinds of light and unlight he witnessed
until his eye-metal rusted away
and now there is no going back no edge no law
no horizon or harbour-wall or rubble breakwater
can keep out this formless from his sightless
nevertheless the grey sea-voice lapping at his skull
even through closed teeth goes on whispering

繆斯啊跟我說說這古老的旅人吧
他發現自己漂流在無底的空間
數不清的星球圈圈環繞他
一如諸神無所事事
所有的光與無光他一一見證
直到眼裡的金屬異物鏽蝕
而此刻再無歸路無邊界無律法
無地平線無海堤或碎石消波塊
抵擋這來自他視盲的渾沌
而仍然海灰色的聲音拍打他的頭顱
甚至穿過緊閉的牙床繼續對他耳語

There was once a stubborn man
searching the earth for the guillemot that speaks
who came at last to the breakneck cliffs and paused
a sleek bird studied him as if to say
you must be that southerner
fated to die of fright if I speak
and a woman once let go of her posture
and shoved herself in a barrel onto the waves
it felt so right to feel her thoughts
hitting her skull

      one person has the character of dust
another has an arrow for a soul
but their stories all end

      somewhere

          in the sea

曾經有個頑固的男人
翻山越嶺尋找那隻會說話的海鴉
終於走到這斷頸崖他停下腳步
一隻羽毛光鮮的鳥打量著他像是在說
你一定是那個南方佬
如果我開口說話你就注定驚嚇而死
也曾經有個女人放下身段
把自己一股腦丟進浪濤
在她的思緒和腦殼相撞的
瞬間她感覺一切都對了

　　　　一人的性情如塵埃
另一人的靈魂像箭矢
但他們的故事都結束

　　　在大海

　　　　　某處

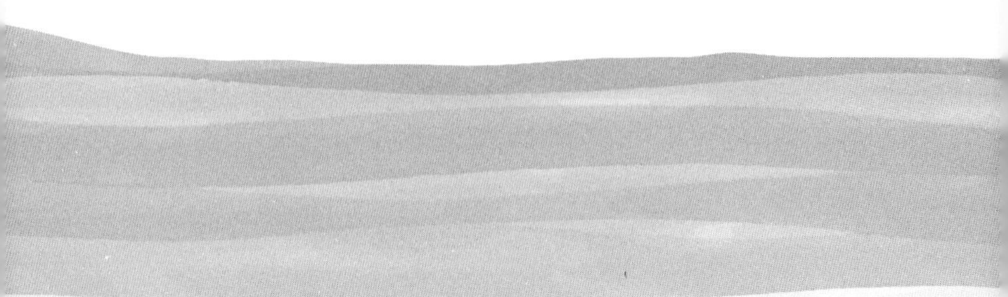

Then we went down to the sea to our black boat
first we dragged the boat into the lively water
and set up mast and sails and drove the sheep on board
then climbed in ourselves depressed crying lukewarm tears
and our hostess who is a goddess long-haired inhuman
but her language is human except when she sings
those bitter grief-songs sent a fair wind
like a friend following a few steps behind
and we busied about securing the ship's tackle
and sat in our places while the wind and the pilot steered us out
all that day the sails at full-stretch drew us over the water
until the sun sank and the roads let slip their shadows
then our boat reached the outer edge of the sea
that feeling of water in its own world moving underneath us
where the blind people live lost under a cloth of fog
and the sun can never burn through it to find them
not when it floats up into space
not when it turns and sinks into the earth
but night always stretches a dark membrane over those people

之後我們就往海往我們的黑船走去
先把船拖進動盪的水
架起船桅船帆把羊群趕上甲板
再各自爬上船情緒低落流下半溫的淚
我們的船主是個長髮女神並非我類
但不唱歌時她說的是人話
她的歌苦澀悲傷隨風飄送
像是隨行在身後幾步的朋友
我們忙著固定船具
各自坐好任憑風和領航員領我們出海
船帆整日張開將我們帶往水域
直到日落道路的蹤影兀自消失
然後我們的船就到了海的外緣
感覺水在它的世界在我們下方挪移
那兒住著一群盲眼人迷失在霧幕下
太陽永不能灼穿霧幕找到他們
霧飄上天空也不能
霧返轉沉入地底也不能
而夜永遠鋪展開一層黑膜覆蓋著那群人

And there I saw the crumpled criminal face of someone
in the fog of her body not knowing what she did
she murdered her husband obscene night
first the gods found out then everyone else
but she her whole soul strangled with horrors
knelt in the bathroom scrubbing and scrubbing
the green of her husband's and her daughter's
disfigured corpse-forms and thought-storms
being lifted up and down as dazed as plankton
it's fine she thought as long as I keep smiling
not mentioning the blood on my nails then nothing
will pass my weakness out between these pointed teeth-posts
not even the murdered one with his last breath
not even necessity will sniff me out

or will she

就在那兒我看到有個人負罪皺癟的臉
在肉體的迷霧中她看不清自己做了甚麼
那悖德的夜晚她謀殺了丈夫
先是諸神發覺異狀然後其他人全知道了
但恐懼扼住了她的魂
她跪在浴室刷洗
她丈夫與女兒變形發青的
屍體而思緒的風暴
像昏亂的蜉蝣上下亂竄
不會有問題的她想只要我保持微笑
不提指甲上的血漬我的軟弱
就不會從這利齒狀的崗哨洩漏出去
即便那氣息奄奄的被害人也無法
即便那命運女神也無法識破我

或者她會嗎

Purpled mind
why go on circling

紫染的意念啊
為甚麼不停繞圈呢

There is a channel where an old sea-god swims
on translucent wings
five miles down in deep unflowered
midnight where it snows and heaps up salt
this goblin-god with ghost-grace frictionlessly moves
or hangs like a pickled heart in the sea-jar

nothing I say sinks down that far

worn-out god can you hear this
look up please from the interstellar hangings
of your under-the-horizon house
there is blood on the tiles
the husband has died struck by his own wife
as he stood naked in the bath

can you hear this

海溝裡有個老海神
以透明的雙翼
在五哩之下幽深無花的
午夜潛泳那兒鹽如堆雪
這精怪帶著鬼魅的優雅
自在漂游
或是像一顆醃漬的心懸浮在海水罐裡

我說的任何話都無法下沉到那麼深

疲憊的神啊祢能聽見嗎
請從水平線下祢屋裡的
星際懸浮物中抬頭看一眼
地板上血跡斑斑
那丈夫赤裸裸站在浴缸之際
遭妻子重擊而死

這祢能聽見嗎

                              No

                    not

        me

別

別是

我

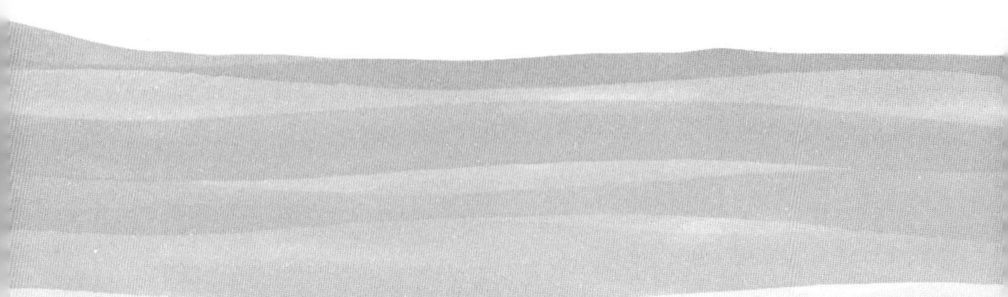

A tired man clinging to a stony out-jut
after a three-hour storm after a ten-year war
clinging to that final handhold thinking
god can you hear this

no

        not

                me

there he sways under the switched-off swinging bulb of the moon
his ship has gone and he is the last man
lashed to the last upright in the roaringnothing thinking
now I really am somebody women are going to love
this quirk I have of outlasting war cloud sickness everything
even water ha! little does he know
what a willpower even now at a hundred miles an hour
is rushing towards his boast with the same wide-open mouth
ready to out-character him and fill his gaping laughter
with salt water now that his handhold
breaks away in his hands and his head drops into the sea

一名精疲力盡的男子抓緊一塊凸出的岩石
歷經了三小時風暴歷經了十年戰火
他抓緊那最後能抓住的想著
神啊這祢能聽見嗎

  別

    別是

      我

就這樣他擺盪在月亮熄滅但搖晃著的燈泡下
船已不知去向他是最後一個活口
被鞭上這咆哮的虛無中最後一個矗立點他想
現在我真是一號人物了女人都會愛上
我的機智一切戰爭烏雲疾病甚至水
都無法擊敗我哈哈他所不知的是
就在這當下某種超意志力正以
時速百哩以同樣大張的嘴衝向他的誇口
用鹽水填滿他張口的大笑屈服他
趁這當下他雙手緊抓不放的
正脫離他雙手而他的頭正栽進海裡

Why is my mind this untranslatable colour of scratchiness and indecision
as of twilight turning into a night accused of corpses
my answer is a swift one a goddess a hundred-mile-an-hour readiness
flying alongside me and I ask you
who would willingly travel over so much water
like a permanent rain-cloud crizzling the sea
so that the waves grow nervous covering up their crimes
but truth will always out and so will

falsehood

為甚麼我的意念毛躁猶豫這無法詮釋的
色彩彷彿暮靄變成製造死亡的夜晚
答案是有一位敏捷的女神正以
時速百哩之姿飛翔在我身邊我問你
誰願意穿越大片水域
像永不散的雨層雲把海弄皺
讓浪變得神經質好掩蓋他們的罪孽呢
但真相必然會浮現而

謊言也會

That goddess pierced by clear-sightedness
falling out of the air as winged and sudden as luck
    like flicking a light-switch
        flash
in the dark of these words she stood here
just a minute ago dead but alive in man's clothes saying
stranger weeping without stopping
cutting off the conversations of those who have a right to be frivolous
it is human to have a name but you seem unsolid somehow
almost too porous to be human I would say
some terrible repetition has eaten into you
as water eats into metal this is what happens
whenever love is mentioned your whole heart liquefies
and the character of water stares out through your eyes
it's as if you were a woman maybe her mind wanders
but it's clear her flesh is damaged in some way
as she drops to her knees and cries and so begins
the simple mineral monologue of

water

女神被明眼看穿
憑空跌落一如運氣展翅乍現
　　　像一開一關的
　　　　　照明
在文字的黑暗中她就站在這兒
就在一分鐘前一身男裝雖死如生說道
異鄉客啼哭個不休
打斷一些饒舌人的輕薄閒話
凡夫皆有姓名而你看來並不扎實
窟窿多得不像人我推測
有些可怕的積習已經蝕入你
就像水侵蝕金屬情況正是如此
一提到愛情你整顆心就會液化
水的特質就從你眼裡流露
彷彿你是個女人或許心思不定
但顯然在跪地哭泣的那一刻肉體
多少受損就這樣開始了
水

單純礦物質的獨白

Who is it saying these things is it only the tide
passing like a rumour over the sea-floor or
who is it keeps silent
when somebody's ring on nobody's hand
sinks like an eye into darkness
and the wind drops
and the water roars itself speechless

who is it speaking she said
my friend
who is it watching me behind your eyelids

是誰在述說這些事呢只是潮汐
謠言般經過海底嗎或者
是誰沉默不語
當大人物的戒指在無名小卒手上
像一隻眼睛沉入黑暗
而風轉弱
而水兀自咆哮無言

是誰正在講話呢她說
我的朋友啊
是誰在你眼瞼後面監視著我呢

Please he said will you please let me sleep

fidgeting under his quilt with one foot touching the floor
you know full well he said this is only the water
talking to us in the voice of amnesia
sometimes with scraping anxious steps
turning over the stones and sometimes
howling the same question over and over
and on his rock that poet shuffles about light-sleeping
every so often answering back

who is it

but for all this for maybe a thousand years
it's been the same answer to the same question

no-one

and on the roof the caretaker scarcely blinks
staring at the sea-sky wondering which way up
he is nailed to the night in case your husband
dressed in his fate but as yet

unmurdered

suddenly appears

他說拜託妳請妳讓我睡一會兒好嗎

單腳著地他在被褥下扭動
妳很清楚他說這只是水
正以失憶的聲音對我們說話
有時摩擦著焦慮的腳步
翻開石頭有時一次次
重複哮吼著同樣的問題
而那詩人在他的岩石上半夢半醒來回走動
偶爾回一句

是誰啊

但對這一切或許千年以來
同樣的問題永遠只有同樣的答案

沒人

而屋頂上那守衛幾乎不眨眼
凝視著海天分不清上方下方
他被釘牢在夜晚以免妳丈夫
雖劫運難逃但一時還

沒死

突然就現身

But for all this for maybe a thousand years
it's been the same answer to the same question

nothing

但對這一切或許千年以來
同樣的問題永遠只有同樣的答案

無

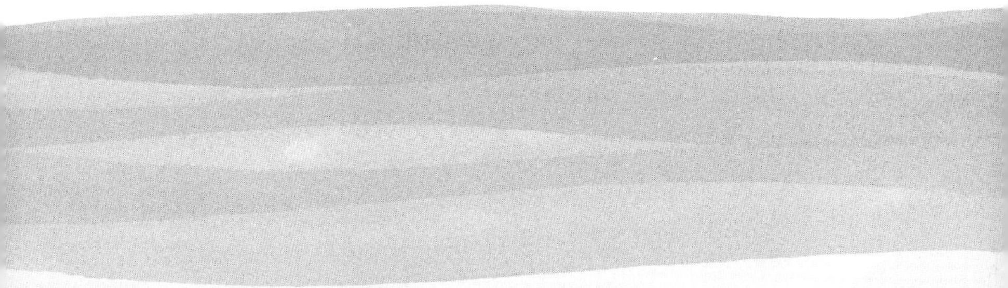

Into which a star a whole unsynchronised solar system
throwing out light like a splash of yellow paint across the night
or else a burning angel falling out of heaven
with briefcase open and his charred documents
drifting about his head descending
from floor to floor he looks liquefied
like a towering sea-plume and finally his feet
which seem to have no difficulty with water
touch down on the horizon without friction

as a seagull sleighs down waves
and wets its stiff wings in the horrible sea-hollows
looking for fish so he swerves and stalls
and finds a woman sitting very still and cold
and wizened with permanent headache on her island
one hand like the shadow of an aeroplane
barely moving over her own blue surface
waves him away she says I know

I know

and the little breezes of her speeches smell like parsley

進入那空無一顆恆星一整座非同步運行的
太陽系拋灑出光芒像黃色油彩濺滿黑夜
或像一名天使著了火從天堂墜下
公事包敞開他焦黑的文件
在頭頂飄散一層層
往下墜他似乎已經液化
像海的一根巨大羽毛而終於雙腳
似乎無礙於水
一無摩擦地觸及水平線

像一隻海鷗滑下波浪
弄濕了僵硬的翅膀在恐怖的海凹處
尋找魚群如此他迅速轉動又停頓
發現一個女人靜坐她的小島上
冷漠乾瘦長期頭痛
一隻手像是飛機陰影
在她藍色的外表上稍稍動了動
示意他走她說我知道

我知道

她說話的細微氣息聞起來像歐芹

You are a messenger and you've come to remove my lover
who is tired of this hotel life you'll find him
sitting on the dunes in tears as always
staring at the sea's round eye of course
Fate has its needle in him nothing can stop him draining away
there seem to be two worlds one is water's
which always finds its level one is love's which doesn't
but is wide a wide field of horrible upheavals
there are gleams mists gusts is he hoping to float himself
on that never-ending to and fro
where the mind no longer belongs to the mind
and a man's shout boomerangs in the wind
the light has no ceiling there are human hands
stuck in the sand like kelp-stalks
and huge cathedrals of waves

a single

moth

struggles under wet sails
but everything warm or weighted always

falls

你是信差受命來帶走我的愛人
他已經厭倦這旅居生涯你會發現他
一如既往坐在沙丘上流淚凝望
海的圓眼而當然命運的針已扎進
他身子他的流失已無可避免
這兒似乎有兩個世界其一是水世界
它永遠找得到平衡其二是情愛世界它不平衡
卻寬闊是一片劇烈動盪的寬闊原野
有微光有薄霧有狂風他是希望自我
流放在那無盡的來去之間嗎
在那兒意念不再屬於意念
一個男子的呼叫聲迴盪在風中
光沒有上限有一些人類的手
像巨藻莖插在沙裡
還有海浪龐然的教堂

孤單單一隻

蛾

掙扎在潮濕的船帆下
但一切有溫度有重量的都會

墜落

So she shrieks and flies up laughing and loud-speakering
and turns and dives unable to be anything for long
and the black wave covers her

所以她尖叫高飛狂笑擴大聲量說話
又轉身俯衝潛水無法持久不變形
而黑色潮浪覆蓋了她

```
C L Y T E M N E S T R A A E G I S T H E U S N O
D M U S M E L I C E R T E S E I D O T H E A P H
E L I O S N O B O D Y I C A R O S L I G E A A E
C Y O N E C A L Y P S O A G A M E M N O N P R O
M O N B A U C I S P H O E N I S S A P H I L O C T
**O R P H E U S** N O B O D Y C I R C E L E U C O T
P E H E L I O S A J A X A T H E N E A N D R O M
Y N O B O D Y **C L Y T E M N E S T R A** A E G I S
O T H E A C A D M U S M E L I E R T E S E I D
O S E I D O N H E L I O S N O B O D Y I C A R O
I A C E Y X A L C Y O N E C A L Y P S O A G A M
E U S P H I L E M O N B A U C I S P H O E N I S S
M N E S T R A O R P H E U S N O B O D Y C I R C
S P E N E L O P E H E L I O S A J A X A T H E N E
```

```
B O D Y O D Y S S E U S L E U C O T H E A C A
O R C Y S E O S A L C Y O N E P O S E I D O N H
G I S T H E U S T H E L X I E P E I A C E Y X A L
O C N E P H I L O M E L P R O T E U S P H I L E
T E T E S C A L Y P S O C L Y T E M N E S T R A
T H E A O R E S T E S G L A U K O S P E N E L O
A C H E H E R M E S P O S E I D O N N O B O D
T H E U S N O B O D Y O D Y S S E U S L E U C
O T H E A P H O R C Y S E O S A L C Y O N E P
S L I G E A A E G I S T H E U S T H E L X I E P E
E M N O N P R O C N E P H I L O M E L P R O T
S A P H I L O C T E T E S C A L Y P S O C L Y T E
C E L E U C O T H E A O R E S T E S G L A U K O
E A N D R O M A C H E H E R M E S P O S E I D O
```

```
C L Y T E M N E S T R A **A E G I S T H E U S** N O
D M U S M E L I C E R T E S E I D O T H E A P H
E L I O S N O B O D Y I C A R O S L I G E A A E
C Y O N E **C A L Y P S O** A G A M E M N O N P R O
M O N B A U C I S P H O E N I S S A P H I L O C T
O R P H E U S N O B O D Y **C I R C E** L E U C O T
P E H E L I O S A J A X A T H E N E A N D R O M
Y N O B O D Y C L Y T E M N E S T R A A E G I S
O T H E A C A D M U S M E L I E R T E S E I D
O S E I D O N H E L I O S N O B O D Y I C A R O
I A C E Y X A L C Y O N E C A L Y P S O A G A M
E U S P H I L E M O N B A U C I S P H O E N I S S
M N E S T R A **O R P H E U S** N O B O D Y C I R C
S P E N E L O P E H E L I O S A J A X A T H E N E
```

```
B O D Y O D Y S S E U S L E U C O T H E A C A
O R C Y S E O S A L C Y O N E P O S E I D O N H
G I S T H E U S T H E L X I E P E I A C E Y X A L
O C N E P H I L O M E L P R O T E U S P H I L E
T E T E S C A L Y P S O C L Y T E M N E S T R A
T H E A O R E S T E S G L A U K O S P E N E L O
A C H E H E R M E S **P O S E I D O N** N O B O D
T H E U S N O B O D Y O D Y S S E U S L E U C
O T H E A P H O R C Y S E O S A L C Y O N E P
S L I G E A A E G I S T H E U S T H E L X I E P E
E M N O N P R O C N E P H I L O M E L P R O T
S A P H I L O C T E T E S **C A L Y P S O** C L Y T E
C E L E U C O T H E A O R E S T E S G L A U K O
E A N D R O M A C H E H E R M E S P O S E I D O
```

```
C L Y T E M N E S T R A A E G I S T H E U S N O
D M U S M E L I C E R T E S E I D O T H E A P H
E L I O S N O B O D Y I C A R O S L I G E A A E
C Y O N E C A L Y P S O A G A M E M N O N P R O
M O N B A U C I S P H O E N I S S A P H I L O C T
O R P H E U S **N O B O D Y** C I R C E L E U C O T
P E H E L I O S A J A X A T H E N E A N D R O M
Y N O B O D Y C L Y T E M N E S T R A A E G I S
O T H E A C A D M U S M E L I E R T E S E I D
O S E I D O N H E L I O S N O B O D Y I C A R O
I A C E Y X A L C Y O N E **C A L Y P S O** A G A M
E U S P H I L E M O N B A U C I S P H O E N I S S
M N E S T R A O R P H E U S N O B O D Y C I R C
S P E N E L O P E H E L I O S A J A X A T H E N E
```

```
B O D Y O D Y S S E U S L E U C O T H E A C A
O R C Y S E O S A L C Y O N E P O S E I D O N H
G I S T H E U S T H E L X I E P E I A C E Y X A L
O C N E P H I L O M E L P R O T E U S P H I L E
T E T E S C A L Y P S O C L Y T E M N E S T R A
T H E A O R E S T E S G L A U K O S P E N E L O
A C H E H E R M E S P O S E I D O N N O B O D
T H E U S **N O B O D Y** O D Y S S E U S L E U C
O T H E A P H O R C Y S E O S A L C Y O N E P
S L I G E A A E G I S T H E U S T H E L X I E P E
E M N O N P R O C N E P H I L O M E L P R O T
S A P H I L O C T E T E S C A L Y P S O C L Y T E
C E L E U C O T H E A O R E S T E S G L A U K O
E A N D R O M A C H E H E R M E S P O S E I D O
```

【歐思華著作】

1. 《石磴間之物》 *The Thing in the Gap-Stone Stile*, 1996
2. 《橡河》 *Dart*, 2002
3. 《樹林等等》 *Woods etc.*, 2005
4. 《夢遊瑟芬河》 *A Sleepwalk on the Severn*, 2009
5. 《雜草與野花》 *Weeds and Wild Flowers*, 2009
6. 《紀念碑》 *Memorial*, 2011
7. 《沉沉醒來》 *Falling Awake*, 2016
8. 《無名人》 *Nobody*, 2019

【歐思華編著】

1. 《雷鳴：101 首詩給星球》 *The Thunder Mutters: 101 Poems for the Planet*, 2005
2. 《湯瑪士・懷特詩選》 *Thomas Wyatt: Selected Poems*, 2008

國家圖書館預行編目資料

無名人/愛莉絲.歐思華(Alice Oswald)著；陳育虹
譯. -- 初版. -- 臺北市：寶瓶文化事業股份有限公
司, 2024.12
　　面；　　公分. -- (Island；339)
　譯自：Nobody
　ISBN 978-986-406-448-9(平裝)
　873.51　　　　　　　　　　　　113018060

寶瓶 AQUARIUS

Island 339

無名人 Nobody

作者／愛莉絲・歐思華 Alice Oswald
譯者／陳育虹

發行人／張寶琴
社長兼總編輯／朱亞君
副總編輯／張純玲
主編／丁慧瑋
編輯／林婕伃・李祉萱
美術主編／林慧雯
校對／林婕伃・陳佩伶・劉素芬・陳育虹
營銷部主任／林歆婕　業務專員／林裕翔　企劃專員／顏靖玟
財務／莊玉萍
出版者／寶瓶文化事業股份有限公司
地址／台北市110信義區基隆路一段180號8樓
電話／(02)27494988　傳真／(02)27495072
郵政劃撥／19446403　寶瓶文化事業股份有限公司
印刷廠／世和印製企業有限公司
總經銷／大和書報圖書股份有限公司　電話／(02)89902588
地址／新北市新莊區五工五路2號　傳真／(02)22997900
E-mail／aquarius@udngroup.com
版權所有・翻印必究
法律顧問／理律法律事務所陳長文律師、蔣大中律師
如有破損或裝訂錯誤，請寄回本公司更換
著作完成日期／二○一九年
初版一刷日期／二○二四年十二月三十日
ISBN／978-986-406-448-9
定價／三四○元

Copyright © 2019 by Alice Oswald
This edition is published by arrangement with United Agents Ltd. through Andrew Nurnberg Associates International Limited.
All rights reserved.
Published by Aquarius Publishing Co., Ltd.
Printed in Taiwan.

寶瓶文化・愛書人卡

感謝您熱心的為我們填寫，對您的意見，我們會認真的加以參考，希望寶瓶文化推出的每一本書，都能得到您的肯定與永遠的支持。

系列：Island 339　書名：無名人

1. 姓名：＿＿＿＿＿＿＿＿＿＿　性別：□男　□女
2. 生日：＿＿＿年＿＿＿月＿＿＿日
3. 教育程度：□大學以上　□大學　□專科　□高中、高職　□高中職以下
4. 職業：＿＿＿＿＿＿＿
5. 聯絡地址：＿＿＿＿＿＿＿＿＿＿＿＿＿＿＿＿＿＿＿
   聯絡電話：＿＿＿＿＿＿＿＿＿＿＿＿＿＿
6. E-mail信箱：＿＿＿＿＿＿＿＿＿＿＿＿＿＿＿＿
   □同意　□不同意　免費獲得寶瓶文化叢書訊息
7. 購買日期：＿＿＿年＿＿＿月＿＿＿日
8. 您得知本書的管道：□報紙／雜誌　□電視／電台　□親友介紹　□逛書店
   □網路　□傳單／海報　□廣告　□瓶中書電子報　□其他
9. 您在哪裡買到本書：□書店，店名＿＿＿＿＿＿＿＿＿＿＿　□劃撥
   □現場活動　□贈書
   □網路購書，網站名稱：＿＿＿＿＿＿＿＿　□其他＿＿＿＿＿
10. 對本書的建議：＿＿＿＿＿＿＿＿＿＿＿＿＿＿＿＿＿＿＿
    ＿＿＿＿＿＿＿＿＿＿＿＿＿＿＿＿＿＿＿＿＿＿＿＿＿
    ＿＿＿＿＿＿＿＿＿＿＿＿＿＿＿＿＿＿＿＿＿＿＿＿＿
11. 希望我們未來出版哪一類的書籍：

（請沿此虛線剪下）

寶瓶
讓文字與書寫的聲音大鳴大放
寶瓶文化事業股份有限公司

亦可用線上表單。

廣告回函
北區郵政管理局登記
證北台字15345號
免貼郵票

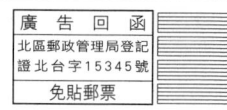

寶瓶文化事業股份有限公司 收

110台北市信義區基隆路一段180號8樓
8F,180 KEELUNG RD.,SEC.1,
TAIPEI.(110)TAIWAN R.O.C.

（請沿虛線對折後寄回，或傳真至02-27495072。謝謝）